EL NOMBRE

All the Fun of the Fair

By Christopher Lillicrap

Finally, it was the day of the Santa Flamingo Fair. Little Juan had been looking forward to it for weeks. He was going with Mama and his pet spider, Tanto.

"Ohh, Mama. . . " said Little Juan. "I'm so excited. I've brought all the money I've saved in my piggy bank." Mama smiled.

"You must promise not to spend all your money, Juan. That would be silly," she said.

"OK, Mama," Little Juan promised.

The Wicked Don Fandango was also at the fair. He heard Little Juan promise not to spend all his savings, but he had other ideas.

"Silly Little Juan, I must think of a plan to get his money, so I can be rich. Ha, ha, ha!" he laughed wickedly.

Manuel was looking after the coconut shy. He was shouting in a big loud voice, "Roll up, roll up, win a coconut. Just throw the balls and knock them. . ." But before he had finished, a hand appeared from behind the stall and grabbed him.

Just then, Juan and Mama spotted the coconut shy.
Juan asked Mama if he could have a go.

"Of course you can, Juan," Mama nodded.

Little Juan thought ten pesos was very expensive.
He also thought that Manuel looked strange, but he
gave him the money anyway. Tanto thought Manuel
looked strange too He wasn't sure that this Manuel
was really Manuel at all. He thought it might be Don
Fandango . . . and he was right.

Tanto tried very hard to tell Little Juan that something was wrong. He jumped up and down trying to get the gerbil's attention. But Little Juan wasn't looking. All he wanted to do was knock off a coconut. Juan hit one with his first throw.

But the coconut didn't fall off. Tanto jumped onto the coconut but he couldn't make it move either.

The coconuts were all stuck down!

Before Little Juan or Mama could say anything, the Wicked Don Fandango threw off his disguise and made his getaway. As he went he pulled half the stall with him. There behind the coconut shy sat poor Manuel. He'd been tied to a chair. Juan rushed over to help.

"It was that Wicked Don Fandango," Manuel explained. When he was untied, Manuel was so pleased he gave Little Juan two free coconuts.

Nearby, Senor Calculo
was standing in front of
the carousel calling,
"Roll up, roll up, have
a ride on the carousel,
only two pesos for a
lovely ride!"

"Oh, I'd love a ride,"
cried Mama.

"I'll pay for you," said
Little Juan, taking some
money from his piggy bank.

"Why, thank you Little Juan,"
Mama said as she climbed onto
one of the wooden horses.

Just then, the Wicked Don Fandango jumped onto the carousel.

"So, Little Juan," he cried, "you wouldn't give me your money at the coconut shy, but you will now! If you don't hand over your piggy bank Mama will be going for a ride she won't forget." He pushed Senor Calculo out of the way. Then he began to push the lever on the carousel from

slow … to fast … to very fast.

The carousel was going round and round at such a speed that Mama had to hold on very tightly to her horse. She was going so fast that her legs flew out and knocked Little Juan and another little gerbil over.

"Oh dear, Tanto," said Little Juan, "I don't know what to do, but I know someone who does."

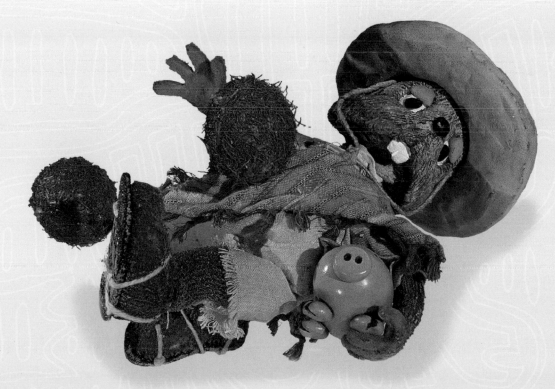

"Yes, it is I, El Nombre,"

the hero cried as he swung
in over the carousel.

"If you want Mama
safe and sound,
First we must stop
her going round!"

El Nombre picked up one of Little Juan's coconuts and hurled it at the Wicked Don Fandango. The shot knocked him right off the carousel. Then he picked up the second coconut and threw it at the lever, knocking it from

very fast . . . to fast . . . to slow.

The carousel came to a sudden stop sending Mama flying. She landed in a heap on the ground.

"What a wonderful fast ride," laughed Mama. "I was really enjoying myself until some fool stopped it!"

"I'd better be off before Mama finds out it was me," El Nombre said as he picked up the Wicked Don Fandango and swung away shouting,

"Well, now my good deed
has been done
Off to jail,
I'll take this one."

"Adios Amigos and keep smiling!"

EL NOMBRE'S PUZZLES

Help El Nombre save the day by working out these puzzles. You might need to go back and check the story to answer some of the questions.

 ◆ How many free coconuts does Juan get given?

 ◆ How many different speed settings are there on the carousel?

 ◆ How many legs does Tanto have?

 ◆ How many coconuts are there on the stall?

◆ Can you read this picture story and work out the puzzle?

Juan has   in his   .

Juan goes on the   which costs   .

How many has he got left?

Then he buys a   which costs   .

How much has he got left now?